SA H GARLAND is a much-loved author and illustrator
wl has published more than 40 books. The daughter of a
pu her and illustrator, she trained as a typographer at the
Lc on College of Printing. Frances Lincoln has published
Eddi Garden, *Eddie's Toolbox*, *Going to Playschool*, *Doing the Garden*,
Go. Swimming, *Coming to Tea*, *Going Shopping*, *Doing Christmas*,
H. g a Picnic, *Doing the Washing*, *Billy and Belle*, *Dashing Dog*,
Pas. Polly and *Azzi in Between*, which was winner of the first
Li Rebels Book Award in 2013 and was also nominated
for the prestigious IBBY Honour Book Award.
Sarah lives in Gloucestershire.

Eddie's Kitchen

and How to Make Good Things to Eat

Sarah Garland

F

FRANCES LINCOLN
CHILDREN'S BOOKS

for Noah and Eve

Text and illustrations copyright © Sarah Garland 2007

First published in Great Britain in 2007 and in the USA in 2008 by
Frances Lincoln Children's Books,
74-77 White Lion Street, London N1 9PF
www.franceslincoln.com

First paperback published in Great Britain and in the USA in 2014

A catalogue record for this book is available from the British Library.

ISBN 978-1-84780-003-9

Printed in China

9 8 7 6 5 4 3 2 1

RRRING! RRRING!

Mum was busy so Eddie answered.

"*Happy birthday to me, happy birthday to me,*" sang Grandad over the phone.

Eddie was surprised. No one had told him that today was Grandad's birthday.

"Happy birthday, Grandad," he said.

"I'll see you at six o'clock for my birthday party," said Grandad. "Bye for now."

"Party?" cried Mum. "Birthday? I've gone and forgotten all about it! And it's two o'clock already!"

"Don't worry, Mum," said Eddie. "I'll help you."

"And me," said Lily.

"But I can't think what to cook! There's Nana and Grandad, and Auntie Maya and all the little ones," said Mum.

"We could make an orange
birthday cake," said Eddie.
"Grandad likes that."

"Spaghetti for me!" said Lily,
and she drew a scribble
which looked like worms.

"Mmmm. That's nice," said Mum.
She wrote down bread,
grated carrot salad, vegetable sticks
with dips, and baked apples.

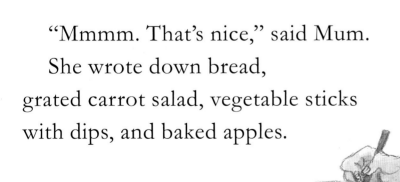

Mum found a box for Eddie to stand on, so he could reach the kitchen table. Then she gave him a bowl for mixing, and a spoon for stirring, and a board for chopping, and a jug for measuring, and scales for weighing. Eddie laid them out and put on his apron.

"I'm ready to cook," said Eddie.

"We'd better make the bread first," said Mum.

Eddie weighed the flour and tipped it into his bowl with teaspoons of salt and sugar and yeast.

Mum had just put some oil and a jug of warm water on the table when there was a **KNOCK! KNOCK!** at the front door.

It was Angie from down the road, and she wanted to show Mum her new baby.

That took some time.

But Eddie knew what to do.

He tipped the oil and the water into his bowl, and mixed everything up, and Lily helped.

When Mum had said goodbye to Angie, she came and looked at Lily.

"What a floury little fairy princess you are," she said, "but that dough looks good."

They each took a piece of dough and
Mum showed them how to make the dough
into a ball, and push it and stretch it
and turn it and stretch it again
until all the lumps had gone
and it was smooth
and silky-soft.

Mum mixed a handful of herbs
into her dough and made a round loaf.

Eddie mixed some crunchy
sunflower seeds into his dough
and made a long loaf.

Lily made her dough into three
sausage shapes.
"Yum," said Lily.
"Wait until it's cooked!" said Mum.

She helped Lily plait her loaf,
then she covered them all
with a cloth and put them
in a warm place above the
oven to rise.

"Now for tomato sauce for the spaghetti," said Mum. "We need one onion, two tins of tomatoes, garlic and a tube of tomato paste."

She had just opened the tins of tomatoes when…

MEEOW! MEEOW!

There was Pusskin, jumping through the cat-flap to drop a mouse on the floor!

"No, thank you!" cried Mum. "We don't want a mouse!"

She chased the mouse around and around the kitchen, and out of the back door into the garden.

That took some time.

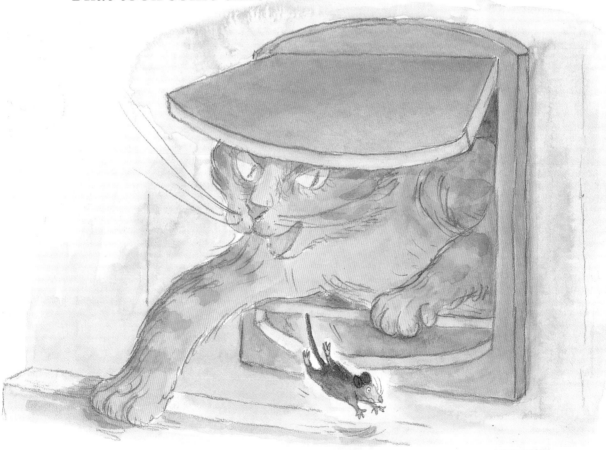

But Eddie knew what to do. He tipped the tomatoes into his mixing bowl, and Lily squeezed the tube of tomato paste, and some of that went into the bowl too.

When Mum came back in, she looked at Lily. "What a tomatoey, floury little fairy princess you are," she said, "but you have both done a good job."

Mum chopped the onion and showed Eddie how to peel the garlic. She cooked that and added the onion to the pan. When they were all soft and yellow, Eddie tipped in the tomato mixture, and soon the good smells in the kitchen made them feel hungry.

"Baked apples next," said Mum, looking at the clock.
"We've got sultanas and dates and butter and brown sugar,
but where can we find some apples?"

Just then there was a **TAP! TAP! TAP!** on the window.

"Hallooo!" called old Mrs Beamish from next door.
"I've got a thorn in my finger. Would you get it out
for me, my dear?"

So Mum got tweezers and a plaster, and sat down
to help old Mrs Beamish.

That took some time.

But Eddie knew what to do. He had seen some apples
lying in the wet grass outside.

They were muddy, so Eddie washed them and Lily
helped him. When they brought the apples into the kitchen,
Mum looked at Lily.

"What a watery, tomatoey, floury little fairy princess
you are," she said, "but those apples are nice and clean."

Mum took out the apple cores and Eddie filled the holes with sultanas and dates, and sprinkled them with sugar and butter and water.

Lily put something else into her apples.

Eddie looked up at the warm place above the oven. "Hey Mum! Look how big the bread has grown!" he said.

"So it has! It's ready to cook," said Mum, and she put the bread and the apples into the hot oven.

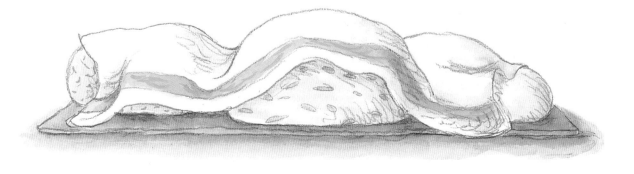

"Now for Grandad's birthday cake," said Mum. "We've got butter and flour and sugar and an orange, but we need four eggs and there's not a single egg in the fridge!"

"Let's look in the hen-house," said Eddie.

But just then, **RRRING! RRRING!** There was the phone again, so Mum had to answer it. It was her friend Martin, who needed cheering up.

That took some time.

But Eddie knew what to do. He took Lily down the garden to the hen-house. They counted the eggs in the nesting-box. One – two – three.

"Grandad's cake needs four eggs!" said Eddie anxiously.

They looked inside the hen-house – no more eggs.

They looked all round the garden – no more eggs.

Eddie ran inside.

Mum had finished talking to Martin and was grating carrots for the salad.

"Three eggs is better than no eggs," she said. "Let's get on with the cake."

Together, they weighed the butter and sugar, and Eddie mixed them up in his bowl while Mum grated the orange peel.

Next, Mum showed Eddie how to crack each egg on the edge of his bowl, and open the egg with his fingers, and tip it into the cake mixture, and mix them in one at a time. One – two – three.

"If we only had just one more egg," said Mum.

They were so busy, they never looked out of the window to see what Lily was doing in the garden.

Lily was playing with her doll,
Bobo Angela.

She thought she would
take her for a walk.

She put her in the pram
and pushed her down the garden.

CLUCK! CLUCK! CLUCK!

Out flew a hen.

And when Lily looked
inside the pram,
what did she find?
A warm white egg!

"Look! Look! Look!"
cried Lily, running indoors.
   "Egg number four! That's
brilliant, Lily," said Eddie.

He showed Lily how to break
the egg into the cake mixture.

   "Well, Lily," said Mum. "What an
eggy, watery, tomatoey, floury little
fairy princess you are, but that
cake mixture looks just right."
   Eddie stirred the flour and
orange peel into the mixture.

Lily stirred in something else
when Eddie wasn't looking.

Mum opened the oven and took out the bread
and the baked apples.

The bread smelt of warm goodness, and the apples
smelt of juicy sweetness.

Eddie tipped the cake mixture into the oiled cake tin,
and Mum put it in the hot oven and shut the door.

"We're doing well," she said.

Now Mum and Eddie and Lily
looked at the clock.
    There was no time to be lost.

Mum cut up a cucumber and
sweet peppers and some celery
into little sticks.

Eddie squeezed half of the
orange to make an orange-juice
syrup for the cake.

Mum mixed up a houmous dip
and a cheesy herb dip.

Eddie and Lily washed
some lettuce for a salad.

Mum filled a big pot with
water for the spaghetti.

Eddie tore up some basil leaves,
ready for the tomato sauce.

Lily opened a packet
of spaghetti.

"We've forgotten to make birthday cards
for Grandad," said Eddie.

"Heavens! So we have!" said Mum.

She cut out some cards while Eddie got out
the painting things.

Mum painted a picture of Pusskin.

Eddie painted a picture of a sunflower.

Lily painted a carrot with fairy wings.

And then the cake was cooked. Out from the oven it came,
and the delicious rich smell filled the kitchen.

Eddie pricked the top of the hot cake with a fork,
then Mum poured the orange syrup over it to soak in
and make it moist and tangy.

At last they were ready to lay the table for the party.

They put out the tablecloth, then some flowers and the cards, and the food, and plates and cups and a big jug of juice.

Mum iced the cake and Eddie put a candle in the middle.

He thought it looked beautiful.

But Mum was looking everywhere for the grated carrots.

"Lily! Have you eaten the carrots?" she said.

"No," said Lily.

"Lily! Come here this minute and let me change you out of your dirty dress," said Mum.

"NO!" said Lily.

"Oh dear," said Mum.

Mum was just putting the spaghetti in the pan
of boiling water, when there was a
KNOCK! KNOCK! KNOCK!
   There, at the front door, were Grandad and Nana,
and Auntie Maya, and all the little ones.
And behind them were Angie and the new baby,
and Mrs Beamish, and Martin, because Mum had
asked them to the party as well.

   "HAPPY BIRTHDAY, GRANDAD," said Eddie.

Soon everyone was talking and laughing,
and eating big bowls of spaghetti and tomato sauce
with chunks of warm bread, and scooping out
the tempting dips with vegetable sticks,
and tasting the sticky, juicy apples.

Nana looked at Mum.

"Did you make all this wonderful food yourself?" she asked.

"Well, Eddie and Lily cooked most of it because I was rather busy," said Mum.

"We cooked it in my kitchen," said Eddie.

Grandad blew out the candle on his cake
and made a secret wish.

He cut a slice and tasted it.

"Mmmm!" he sighed. "How did you know, Eddie,
that orange-and-carrot cake is my favourite cake in
the whole world?"

"So *that's* where the carrots went!"
said Eddie, and he looked at Lily.

"Princesses ALWAYS like
carrots," said Lily.

How to make Eddie's food

Here are recipes for the food cooked for Grandad's birthday party. Each dish is versatile, delicious and fun to make, involving a child from start to finish.

Spaghetti with Rich Tomato Sauce

Few children can resist pasta, and for this simple sauce even the smallest child can measure the oil and tomato puree, peel the garlic and tear up the basil leaves. This recipe serves four to six people.

Ingredients

3 tablespoons olive oil
2 garlic cloves, finely sliced
1 medium onion, chopped
2 400g (14.5 oz) tins (cans) plum tomatoes
2 tablespoons concentrated tomato puree
½ teaspoon white sugar

salt and pepper
a handful of fresh basil leaves, roughly torn, and/or a teaspoon of thyme or oregano or dried mixed herbs.
450g dried spaghetti
Grated parmesan or other cheese (optional)

Method

• Heat the oil in a deep frying pan and fry the sliced garlic until just golden.
• Turn down the heat, add the chopped onion and simmer slowly for 15 minutes, stirring occasionally, until they are soft but not brown.
• Stir the tomatoes into the pan, chopping them roughly, with the tomato puree, sugar, salt, pepper and herbs (but not basil leaves).
• Simmer over a low heat, uncovered, for about 20 minutes, stirring occasionally, until the sauce has reduced and thickened.
• Taste for seasoning and stir in the basil leaves.

• To cook the spaghetti, bring a large pan of water to a fast boil and stir in a tablespoon of salt. Stand the spaghetti in the pan and press gently down with a wooden spoon until it is submerged. Stir to separate the strands. Bring the water back to the boil and stir frequently until cooked. As soon as a strand feels slightly tender, and while it is still just firm to the bite, drain the pasta immediately in a colander. Tip the drained pasta straight into the hot sauce. Mix sauce and pasta thoroughly, using two forks, and serve in a warm dish, with grated cheese on the side.

Note: This sauce makes a wonderful pizza topping too. Spread it on a pizza base made by following the bread recipe on the next page. Sprinkle with cheese and bake for 20-25 minutes at 400F/205C/Gas mark 6.

Crusty White Bread

Bread-making is a hands-on pleasure, especially for children. Don't be daunted by the amount of time it takes to produce a warm crusty loaf — most of this time is spent allowing the dough to rise. In the story, Eddie's bread had to be made quickly, but in this recipe the dough is given two periods of rising which gives the loaf a more open texture.

Ingredients

1 kilo (4½ cups) white bread flour
2 heaped teaspoons dried quick yeast
2 heaped teaspoons white sugar

2 heaped teaspoons salt
2 tablespoons light olive oil or sunflower oil
Warm water

Method

• Tip the flour into a big mixing bowl with the yeast, sugar, salt and oil. (I have suggested quick yeast which is easily available. Check the instructions on the packet.)

• Pour about 550ml (2½ cups) warm water into the mixture and stir it around until it makes a soft dough. Add a little water if it is too dry.

• Tip it out, and start to knead the dough, sprinkling with a little flour if it is too sticky.

• Push and stretch the dough away from you with the heel of your hand, then gather and roll it back into a ball. Give the ball a quarter turn and stretch it away again. Repeat for at least seven minutes. You can also press into the dough with the heel of your hand and fold it back over itself, then turn and repeat.

• The dough should now feel smooth and springy under your fingers. Put a teaspoonful of oil into the mixing bowl, roll the dough around in it, cover with a cloth, and put it in a warm, draught-free place to rise for about 45 minutes to an hour until it is nearly doubled in size.

• Now knead it briefly to knock the air out of it, and divide into three.

• Shape into loaves, as in Eddie's story. Lay the three loaves on a well-oiled baking sheet, cover them with a cloth, and put to rise again in a warm place for 30 to 45 minutes until nearly doubled in size.

• Bake in a hot oven at 425F/ 220C/Gas mark 7 and after 15 minutes reduce the heat to 400F/205C/Gas mark 6.

• Another 10 minutes and the loaves should be ready, with a crisp golden crust which sounds hollow when tapped.

• Cool on a rack.

Note: Halve these quantities and roll out after the second rising for a pizza base.

Orange drizzle cake (with carrot)

This is a moist and delicious cake. Children can help at every stage, but soften the butter very well before you begin, to make it easier for them to beat.

Ingredients

250g (1 cup) butter
150g (¾ cup) caster sugar
4 eggs
1 orange (juice squeezed, rind grated)
100g (½ cup) finely grated carrot
250g (1 cup) self raising flour

for the syrup
50g (½ cup) granulated sugar
2 tablespoons orange juice

Method

• Set the oven to 325F/160C/Gas mark 3.
• Beat the softened butter and the sugar with a wooden spoon until creamy and smooth.
• Beat in the eggs, one by one. The first may curdle the mixture slightly – add a tablespoonful of the flour and beat hard. The other eggs will mix in more easily.
• Stir in the grated orange rind, grated carrot and 2 tablespoons of orange juice.
• Use a metal spoon to fold in the flour lightly and thoroughly.
• Oil the cake tin. (I tip in a splash of sunflower oil and spread it around with my fingers.)
• Put the cake mixture in the tin and bake for about 40 minutes. Check halfway through and turn the heat down if the cake is looking too dark round the edges.
• Carefully press the centre of the hot cake – it is cooked when it feels firm and resilient and has shrunk slightly from the sides of the tin.
• Take the cake out of the oven, leave it in the tin, and prick the top lightly all over with a fork.
• Mix the syrup ingredients and pour them immediately over the hot cake. Leave the cake in the tin until the syrup is absorbed (about 10 minutes).
• Take out of the tin and cool on a rack.
• Although the cake is perfect as it is, you can ice it with 150g (¾ cup) icing sugar beaten with about 2 tablespoons of orange juice, and decorate it with candied fruit or peel.

Note: This basic cake mixture can be used (minus the carrot and orange) for lemon drizzle cake (use 2 lemons), chocolate cake (add 4 tablespoons grated plain chocolate), coffee and walnut (add 2 tablespoons instant coffee dissolved in a little boiling water, and a handful of chopped walnuts).
Or put spoonfuls of any of these mixtures into greased bun tins or paper cases and bake for about 10 minutes for fairy cakes (cupcakes).

Baked and buttery apples

Use eating apples such as Coxes, as they will hold their shape when baked.
Cooking apples may dissolve into a foam.

Ingredients
1 medium to large eating apple per person
1 date to each apple
Sultanas
Butter
Light brown sugar

Method
• Choose a baking dish which is large enough to hold the apples in a single layer,
butter it generously and sprinkle with several spoonfuls of sugar.
• Core the apples and score them lightly around their waists. Stuff each one
with a few sultanas and a date, and top with half a teaspoon of sugar and a flake of butter.
• Pour in a centimetre (½ inch) of water and bake for about 30 minutes at 350F/160C/Gas mark 3,
basting occasionally with their thick, bubbling, buttery juices.
• Take out the dish and let the apples cool for a few minutes.

Note: Eat warm with vanilla ice-cream. Don't stuff with carrots!

Cooking Together

Toddlers love to be involved in the making of snacks and meals. With a box to stand on
at the table or kitchen counter, they will watch what you are doing, demand to help
and make a mess. Give them small jobs to do, and give them little tastes of the food
you are cooking. Let them discover new flavours, smells and textures of food.

Children may get impatient and snappy when they are tired, so try not to cook together
too late in the day. Don't make them feel they have to help make a dish from start to finish.
Explain that what they have done is an important part of the production of a meal.

Choosing recipes together, making lists, and shopping for food, all help to spark a child's
enthusiasm. Go to farm shops or farmers' markets together, where they can experience
unwrapped, seasonal produce. Buy organic food when possible, especially dairy food,
flour, fruit and vegetables.

Children who enjoy cooking their food will be far more likely to be interested in
eating it, especially if you are sitting down and eating the meal together, and can
discuss successes and failures. And they are likely to become adventurous cooks,
ready to experiment with new and unusual food – and to become adventurous
eaters too – and that is a lasting pleasure.

COLLECT ALL THE *EDDIE* BOOKS BY SARAH GARLAND, PUBLISHED BY FRANCES LINCOLN CHILDREN'S BOOKS

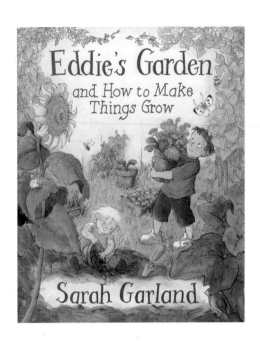

EDDIE'S GARDEN

"Offers plenty of information in a gentle, accessible way." *Early Years Educator*

"Clearly and delightfully told, with lively characters and colourful illustrations, this gentle story is also packed full of information on how to grow a garden like Eddie's for yourself." *LoveReading4Kids*

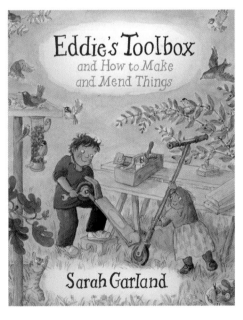

EDDIE'S TOOLBOX

"This exceptional book will inspire children to make and mend for themselves. An all-round winner!" *IBBY Link*

Frances Lincoln titles are available from all good bookshops.
You can also buy books and find out more about your favourite titles,
authors and illustrators on our website: www.franceslincoln.com